Aberdeenshire
COUNCIL

Aberdeenshire Library and Information Service
www.aberdeenshire.gov.uk/libraries
Renewals Hotline 01224 661511

Evans

A L I S

First published in the UK in 2010 by
Evans Brothers Limited
2A Portman Mansions
Chiltern Street
London
W1U 6NR

This edition © 2010 Evans Brothers Limited

First published in the USA in 2009 by
Marshall Cavendish Corporation,
Tarrytown, NY
Text and Illustration copyright © 2009 by Steve Shreve

British Library Cataloguing in Publication Data
Shreve, Steve.
    The Bogey Man, or, A good argument for not picking your nose.
    (The adventures of Charlie)
    1. Charlie (Fictitious character: Shreve) Juvenile fiction.
    2. Monsters Juvenile fiction.
    3. Adventure stories.
    4. Children's stories.
    I. Title II. Series III. Good argument for not picking your nose
    813.6-dc22

ISBN-13: 9780237542870

Printed in China

The ADVENTURES of CHARLIE

The Bogeyman

OR
A GOOD ARGUMENT FOR NOT PICKING YOUR NOSE

by

Steve Shreve

t was late one Thursday night, and everyone was getting ready for bed. Everyone except for Charlie – he hated bedtime.

Charlie ran around the house in his underwear, as his poor, exhausted father chased him with his toothbrush.

But after a while, even Charlie became tired. So he brushed his teeth, put on his pyjamas, and went to the kitchen to feed his dog, Banjo.

They were out of dog food, so
Charlie fed Banjo some leftover
hotdogs and cabbage he found at
the back of the fridge.

Banjo didn't seem to mind.

Finally, Charlie climbed into bed, turned out the lights, pulled up the covers, and fell fast asleep.

But later, a loud noise woke him right up – **BANG!**

What's that? he wondered. Charlie went to check it out.

He looked in his cupboard.

He looked in his toy chest.

He even looked through the big, stinky pile of dirty clothes in the corner.

Well, he thought, *I've checked just about everywhere. Everywhere but under my bed.*

He tiptoed across the room, bent down, and *slooowly* lifted up the covers.

Charlie jumped back!

A slimy, bug-eyed monster
leaped out.

"BLEEARGH!" he roared. "I'm the
Bogeyman! And now that you've
found me, I'm going to eat you!"

"The Bogeyman?" Charlie exclaimed.
"Don't be silly, the Bogeyman
doesn't exist!"

"I certainly do exist!" replied
the Bogeyman.

Charlie was puzzled.

"Wait a minute," Charlie said.
"What are you doing under my
bed, anyway?"

"Hey, I just go where the bogeys are — and someone's been wiping a lot of them under this bed. Besides, I need a place to make phonecalls, take naps, and do my laundry."

"I never really thought about all that before," said Charlie.

"Yeah, well, a lot of nose-pickers like you don't," the Bogeyman replied. "Now hold still so I can eat you."

"Well, you *could* eat me," said Charlie, thinking fast, "but I am pretty little."

The Bogeyman looked closely at Charlie. "Hmmm," he said. "You are a bit small."

"But my dog's big and fat," Charlie added. "And he never exercises, so he's probably good and tender."

"I suppose that would be okay," said the Bogeyman. "I only had a light lunch, and I am *very* hungry."

So the Bogeyman crept into the living room, where Charlie's dog, Banjo, was snoring loudly.

The Bogeyman quietly snuck up behind Banjo. He opened his mouth as wide as he could and prepared to gobble up the dog in one big, bogery bite.

But just then, a tiny little noise came out of Banjo — "Poot."

"What's that . . ."

". . . horrible, horrible smell?"
cried the Bogeyman.

Banjo had just farted.

"PEE-YEW! What have you been feeding that dog?"

"Hot dogs," replied Charlie, "with cabbage."

The Bogeyman tried to get away from the stink, but it was too late. His eyes began to water, and his stomach began to heave.

"I think I'm going to be sick!" And with that, the Bogeyman raced for the door . . .

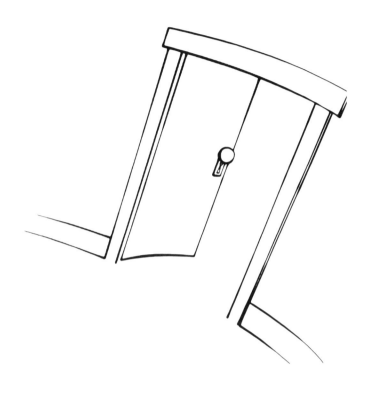

. . . and straight for the bathroom.

He leaned over the toilet . . .

. . . and Charlie took this opportunity
to sneak up behind him, push
him in, and pull the handle –

WHOOSH!

The Bogeyman was sucked
head-first down into the sewer system.

Charlie always knew that the toilet
would come in handy one day.

Charlie headed back to his bedroom.

But before going to sleep, he took a few minutes to clean up under his bed.

Just in case.

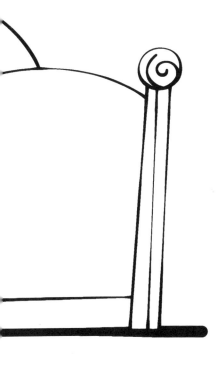